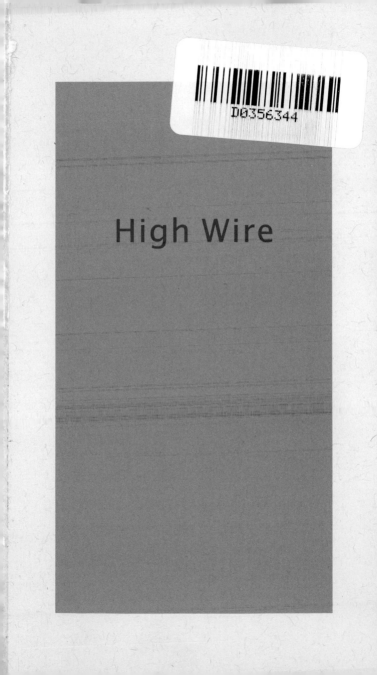

High Wire

High Wire

Melanie Jackson

Orca currents

ORCA BOOK PUBLISHERS

Library and Archives Canada Cataloguing in Publication

Jackson, Melanie, 1956-
High wire / Melanie Jackson.
(Orca currents)

Issued also in electronic formats.
ISBN 978-1-4598-0237-7 (BOUND).--ISBN 978-1-4598-0236-0 (PBK.)

I. Title. II. Series: Orca currents
PS8569.A265H53 2012   jc813'.6   C2012-902229-2

First published in the United States, 2012
Library of Congress Control Number: 2012938159

Summary: High-wire walker Zack
has to solve a mysterious theft at the youth circus.

*Orca Book Publishers is dedicated to preserving the environment and has
printed this book on paper certified by the Forest Stewardship Council®.*

Orca Book Publishers gratefully acknowledges the support for its
publishing programs provided by the following agencies: the Government
of Canada through the Canada Book Fund and the Canada Council for the Arts,
and the Province of British Columbia through the BC Arts Council
and the Book Publishing Tax Credit.

Cover photography by Dreamstime.com

ORCA BOOK PUBLISHERS
PO BOX 5626, Stn. B
Victoria, BC Canada
V8R 6S4

ORCA BOOK PUBLISHERS
PO BOX 468
Custer, WA USA
98240-0468

www.orcabook.com
Printed and bound in Canada.

15 14 13 12 • 4 3 2 1

To Bart,
who catches me when I fall.

Chapter One

The thin black line stretched out in front of me.

I stood on the ledge. The spotlight was fixed on me, hot, white and bright. I couldn't see the opposite ledge. I couldn't see the crowd below, watching to see if I'd make it across.

All I saw was that thin black line going from the spotlight into darkness.

The line was all that mattered to me.

I inhaled deeply. I set my shoulders back. I flexed my arm and chest muscles. I extended my arms sideways to transfer my weight away from my chest, my center of being. The secret to high-wire walking is to place your weight at your sides. It takes a lot of practice and many falls into the safety net to get it right. By nature, people bend their weight forward when they move.

I stepped on the wire. I placed each leather-slippered foot sideways, penguin style. I curved each sole to fit the line.

The audience was dead quiet. Without realizing it, people suck in their breath during a risk act. It's instinctive. They're afraid of making the slightest noise. Of disturbing the walker.

They don't get that nothing else exists when you're on the line. It's just you above the world. You make your deal with gravity, and you and the air are one.

I thought of Philippe Petit, the most famous wire walker in history. New York City, 1974, Petit crossed a steel cable stretched between the Twin Towers of the World Trade Center, a quarter of a mile up. For forty-five minutes, he walked that wire back and forth *eight times*.

As I walked forward, I imagined how Petit must have felt. The sun above, the sky all around. The clean, sweet air. For the minutes it took him to cross, he'd been alone, hassle-free.

That was the appeal of high wire for me. I liked being on my own.

A couple of years ago, my folks died in a plane crash. I moved from our ranch in Alberta to Maple Ridge, near Vancouver, to live with my Aunt Ellie.

My aunt wasn't used to having a kid around. She thought I needed fussing over. I knew she meant well, but it got annoying.

Luckily, she was busy much of the time running her organic-foods store.

I hung around the community center. I'd always been into fitness, anyway. I liked pressing weights and pacing the treadmill.

I noticed there was a juggling class. I had nothing better to do, so I signed up.

The teacher, a retired circus performer named Shecky, grunted at my balance, my self-control. It took me a while to realize grunting was Shecky's way of showing wild enthusiasm.

One day he fastened a wire, three feet off the ground, between two metal height-adjustable ladders.

If you can juggle, you can walk the line. A lot of high-wire walkers start out as jugglers. Philippe Petit did.

That got my attention. *Philippe who?*

Shecky grunted and loaned me a DVD about Petit's Twin Tower walk. Shecky explained, *You'll see that he uses the same principles of balance on the wire as in juggling: weight to the sides.*

At first, every time I walked the wire, Shecky danced around me, making weird faces and waving his arms. He wanted to see if he could distract me. He even did cartwheels.

But he never got to me. *Huh*, he grunted.

After a while he gave up and just kept raising the wire.

One day he told me Circus Sorelli, the summer youth troupe, was looking for a new wire walker. I auditioned, and I got the job.

And now, here I was, seventy-five feet above the ground, on my first night as a Circus Sorelli performer.

Someday I'd be a quarter mile up, like Philippe Petit.

Because nothing got to me. I never wavered. I had complete self-control. It was just me and the line.

The spotlight tracked me across the high wire. I heard people letting their breaths out. They realized I knew what I was doing. They sensed I was comfortable on the wire.

The spotlight crept to the opposite ledge. Five more steps and I'd be there.

This was the most dangerous part of a high-wire walk. You see the opposite ledge, your finish line. You could so easily let down your guard. You could relax and let some of your weight go forward, instead of at your sides.

And you'd fall, *whissssh!*, into the safety net. Into failure. Into humiliation.

Not me. I kept my bargain with gravity. I stepped onto the ledge.

The crowd roared their approval. They stood up, clapped and whistled.

I climbed down the ladder. The spotlight was already swooping down to high-beam the Circus Sorelli clowns.

One by one, the three clowns made their entrance on tiny bicycles. Their routine was to throw water-filled balloons at each other, crash into the ringside wall and do other goofy stuff.

In the shadows, crew members hurried into the ring to fold up the safety net. They moved lightning-fast.

Keeping out of their way, I walked toward change rooms behind the ring so I could switch my leather slippers for runners. I didn't want to wear the slippers down by walking too much on ground.

"That's your act, Freedman? Your mommy and daddy bribe the ringmaster?"

It was the third clown, Cubby Donnell, who was waiting in the shadows for his cue.

I shared a trailer with Cubby. From day one, he'd been giving me a hard time. I was so busy practicing and working out that I'd pretty much ignored him. Till now.

He probably didn't know about my folks being dead. It didn't matter. This time he'd got to me.

I wheeled round and glared into his painted face. I grabbed his floppy collar. "Maybe you'd like to try being up in the air too," I invited.

Twisting the collar, I lifted Cubby off the ground.

In the spotlight, the second clown smashed his tiny bike into a tub of yellow paint. He dived headfirst into the tub. The crowd screamed with laughter.

This was Cubby's cue to bike into the ring. I didn't let go. I'd been feeling good about the standing O, and he'd tried to wreck that.

He thrashed around, but I kept my grip on his collar. I smiled into his neon red grin.

"What's your problem with me, Cub?"

The spotlight beamed, empty, into the ring. Cubby was supposed to be there. The crowd murmured. People knew something was wrong.

Cubby was sweating through his clown makeup. "Lemme go. I'm sorry for hassling you...*Zen*."

Zen was the nickname I had at Circus Sorelli for being so calm on the wire.

I dropped Cubby. He staggered sideways. He was too stunned to climb on his bike. Instead, holding it by the handlebars, he stumbled into the spotlight.

The crowd thought this weaving-around entrance was part of Cubby's act, and applauded.

I didn't know what Cubby's problem was.

As he biked around the edge of the spotlight, he passed close to me and hissed, "I'm not through with you, Freedman. Not by a long shot."

Chapter Two

I pushed through the black curtain. Usually the next performers were lined up behind it. They did stretching exercises or watched the ring act on closed-circuit TV.

This time they stood in a huddle. At the sight of me, they stepped aside. One of the gymnasts, Whitney Boothroyd, was holding a bundle of blankets.

"Hey, Zack," Whitney greeted me. Her dark eyes shone. "Congratulations. Your aunt dropped off a present. Someone to keep you company, she said."

Whimpering came from the blankets.

Oh *no*, I thought.

Aunt Ellie had been saying she wished we had more family. More relatives to keep me company.

I could only gape at the bundle, which was struggling inside the blanket. I couldn't believe it. Aunt Ellie had gone and adopted a baby. I thought that was crazy for a woman in her mid-fifties.

"Don't you want to hold him?" Whitney urged.

"No," I said. "He's got to be returned." Vague images of bundling the kid into a courier package flashed through my mind.

Okay, I might have to rethink the method of transportation. But there was no way I wanted a baby brother.

I realized the bundle wasn't a baby when it stopped whimpering and started barking.

The dog poked its face out of the blanket and looked around.

"Sooo cute!" Whitney cooed.

"Are you kidding?" I said distastefully. The pooch's face was a bunch of flabby rolls. His mouth was turned down like he was sulking. His body was too small for his head.

On my parents' ranch, I'd had a border collie named Thelma. She was strong and energetic, able to run for miles. Thelma lived with another rancher now. I missed her a lot.

That's what busybody Aunt Ellie had been thinking. She would replace Thelma...with this little yapper. Why couldn't she leave me alone?

"He's a French bulldog cross," Whitney was saying. "Some terrier in him, I'm guessing. Just adorable."

13

The kids laughed at my sour expression.

Somebody asked, "Hey, Zack. What's his name?"

I shook my head. "I dunno." I didn't want to name the thing. Giving it a name might make me responsible for him.

"He's just some pooch," I said.

"Hi, Pooch," Whitney crooned.

The ringmaster and circus owner, Mr. Sorelli, stomped into the room, his black eyebrows smashed into a scowl. This was more or less his permanent expression. He wore a glittery red ducktail-type jacket with matching jodhpurs and a top hat.

He shouted, "What's going on? The idea is to stay *quiet* during other performers' acts. The audience out there can hear you, right up to the top bleacher."

They'd be able to hear Sorelli too. But no one had the nerve to point that out.

"Zack's aunt gave him this little sweetie," Whitney said. She was planting kisses on Pooch's ugly face. I wondered if her eyesight was bad.

She handed the dog to me. The clown act was finishing, and she was on next.

The ringmaster switched his baleful gaze to me. His bullet-like eyes narrowed. "This is a circus, not a zoo, Zachary. Get rid of the mongrel. Now."

I took Pooch into the guys' dressing room. I opened my gym bag and changed shoes.

Pooch stuck his head in the gym bag and sniffed around. When he emerged, he was holding one of my leather slippers in his teeth.

I was mad, but I knew to pry the slipper away from him slowly. You can make a dog let go of anything if he thinks you don't want it. My border collie had been that way.

Any similarity between Thelma and Pooch ended there. I viewed Pooch's ugly face and squat body. Thelma had sure been better-looking.

I carried Pooch out back of the big top. I set him down. He promptly took a dump.

"Why me?" I asked him.

By now it was dark outside, but I decided I'd better do the good-citizen thing. The way my luck was going, Sorelli would step *splat* into Pooch's poop. I scooped his business into a bag and shoved the whole thing into the nearest trash bin.

Pooch's trusting brown eyes watched me.

"Don't get any ideas. Tomorrow I'm taking you back to Aunt Ellie. I'm stuck with you tonight."

He wagged his tail.

I walked Pooch to my trailer. All the circus performers and crew lived onsite. The crew had set up the big top in Vancouver's Vanier Park near Kits Beach. The huge tent would be a red-and-white-striped city landmark until Labour Day. Concession and souvenir stands crammed the field in front of the big tent. The trailers were parked behind it.

Pooch trotted along close to me like we were old pals. Dumb dog didn't know he wasn't wanted.

I figured he'd need some water by now. We didn't have a bowl in the trailer, so I rinsed out the toothbrush glass and filled it up with water. Pooch stuck his snout into the glass. He glugged the water back.

At least he wasn't fussy.

I got out my cell phone. I needed to talk to Aunt Ellie. I would explain that Circus Sorelli couldn't have any animals. Not so much as a pet goldfish.

The ringmaster had told me this during orientation.

He'd also said that fewer and fewer circuses these days featured animals. It wasn't so much that elephants and lions were dangerous. They could be trained.

People were the danger. There were hundreds of horror stories about animals being mistreated, like getting whipped or jammed into too-small cages. In the United Kingdom, they've passed a law banning animal acts in circuses.

I wanted to let Aunt Ellie know all this, so her feelings wouldn't be hurt.

And so she would butt out. I had to get Pooch back to Aunt Ellie. Let her deal with him.

But I never got a chance to phone her. Instead I found a text message: *I adopted the pup from the pound. A replacement for Thelma! BTW, I'm off to the Okanagan on business. See you next week.*

She was out of town.

And Sorelli wanted Pooch gone now.

I covered my face with my hands and let out an agonized groan. Thanks a lot, Aunt Ellie.

What was I going to do?

Chapter Three

"Something wrong, Zen?"

Cubby strolled into the trailer. He'd toweled some of his makeup off, but a white sheen remained. It made him look ghostly or badly in need of a blood transfusion.

I didn't have time to reply. Pooch bared his teeth and growled at him.

Cubby jumped.

The dog advanced. Cubby backed away, frightened.

I laughed. It was funny to see this little yapper taking on a tall guy like Cubby.

I picked Pooch up. "Pooch, Cubby," I introduced them. "Pooch is just visiting. I'll take him for a walk. That should settle him down."

As I walked out, I got a foul look from Cubby. I guessed I shouldn't have laughed. I hadn't improved relations between us any.

Intermission had started. I had time to walk Pooch around the circus grounds.

Pooch ran in circles around me. This was his way of urging me to get a move on.

On the other side of the big top, a giant billboard of Sorelli looked down on us. This smiling cartoon ringmaster raised his top hat beside big red letters: *Circus Sorelli—The Be Happy Place!*

It was a cheerful summer landmark for the city.

It was all in your point of view, of course. For us performers, the huge sign meant the ringmaster was always watching us.

I scratched Pooch behind his ears. Pooch gave a pleased *woof*!

Once we got outside the big top, Pooch trotted calmly along beside me. I bought a burger from the concession stand. I broke it up into pieces, and set it on the ground on a paper plate. Pooch gobbled it up.

People hurried past, seeking out their own snacks or buying souvenirs, like Circus Sorelli Ts or red-sequined ringmaster jackets.

I breathed in the salt-tangy air. Mixed up in it was the baked-vanilla aroma of cotton candy from another concession stand. I always thought it was weird how cotton candy smelled better than it tasted.

Once Pooch finished the burger, we walked around some more. People were gabbing excitedly about the acts they'd seen.

A couple of boys were talking about me. "Didja see how slick the wire guy was?"

They were looking at a huge placard with photos of all the performers.

"What's his name? Let's find him." They squinted at the photos.

I waited to hear them say *Zack Freedman*. Maybe one day I'd be blasé about getting recognized. For now I was a First of May. Circus folk called new performers First of Mays because circuses traditionally open on May 1.

"Yeah, there he is! Jacob Donnell."

Huh? I stepped over to peer at the placard.

Sure enough, under the words *High-Wire Performer* was a photo of Cubby.

I stared at Cubby with his toothy smile.

So Cubby had been on the wire before me. I guessed they hadn't printed new placards yet.

I recalled the ringmaster saying that the previous wire walker, Jacob, seemed too tense on the wire. Sorelli told me you couldn't enjoy watching him.

Sorelli always called kids by their formal names. Jacob…*Cubby*.

I hadn't clued in, but now I got why Cubby was so hostile. Why he kept razzing me.

He resented me for getting his job.

The two boys were watching me curiously. I gave a mock bow. "I'm your friendly wire walker. Zack Freedman."

The boys rolled their eyes. One scoffed, "Yeah, right. Dream on, buddy."

At first I was annoyed. Then it struck me as funny. I laughed.

The boys looked nervous. They probably thought I was a nutter. They walked away, muttering.

Pooch and I walked around some more. We got a few disapproving glances. The No Animals Allowed sign greeted people at the gate.

I told Pooch, "Too bad you're such a squirt. Otherwise you could pass for a seeing-eye dog. What's the point of small dogs, anyway? Huh?"

Pooch just looked up at me, tongue hanging out. He was happy.

Dumb dog.

We would have got more looks if I'd been wearing a clown outfit, or a bodysuit like the acrobats and trapeze artists. People would stop and gape at someone they thought was a performer.

But I wasn't into costumes. Even for my act, I wore only lightweight painter pants and a Circus Sorelli T-shirt.

I explained to Pooch, "When Philippe Petit walked between the towers, he wore street clothes. I'm with him. You don't need a costume to live out a dream. You need what's inside you. Determination. Self-control."

Pooch was busy sniffing a half-eaten cotton candy. Some idiot had dropped it on the ground.

I didn't want Pooch to eat it—that molten sugar would wreck his teeth.

Without thinking, I whistled for him: *Hooo-eee*. It was the way I'd whistled for Thelma.

It must be universal dog language. Pooch pricked up his ears. He left the cotton candy and trotted after me.

In the back of the big top, I tied Pooch to a tent pole. I used the skipping rope I kept in my gym bag.

I was up next with my juggling act. Sorelli was out in the ring, warming the audience up for the second half of the show. We could hear his groaners.

"How hot is it today? I'll tell ya. I was up on Cypress Mountain, and the caps were melting." Pause. "The caps on my *teeth*! Now *that's* hot!"

Whitney walked into the waiting area. She was done for the night, but performers often hung around to chat. She bent down to pet Pooch and coo over him.

I left my spot at the head of the line and joined her. In a low voice I said, "Tell me about Cubby—how he lost the wire job."

She straightened, her dark eyes somber. She glanced around to make sure the others weren't listening. "I can't talk about it, Zack. If I do, *I'll be cursed!*"

Chapter Four

I stared at Whitney. Then I remembered circus superstitions. It was bad luck to talk about another performer's mistakes. It was also bad luck to bring peacock feathers to a circus or fall asleep inside the big top.

This last superstition actually made sense at one time. In the early 1900s, before bleacher-type seats, crews piled dirt to make a raised ring. They wanted to be sure everyone could see. When performers jumped around, the dirt sometimes collapsed, burying front-row audience members alive. So, at the start of a circus performance, the ring-master would warn the audience not to fall asleep.

"I'll protect you from any curses," I promised Whitney. "I just want to know why Cubby has been hassling me since I got here."

We could hear Sorelli still cracking jokes. After that, he'd get into warn-ings about shutting off cell phones and not using cameras. We had a couple of minutes.

Whitney sighed and nodded. "Okay. Well, this is Cubby's third year with the circus. In his first year he was part of the clown act. Last year he got the wire job. He thought the wire was so cool— not goofy, like the clown act.

"But after the summer was over, Sorelli said Cub didn't have the flair to be a professional wire walker. He put Cubby back to being a clown."

Whispering now, Whitney added, "Cubby was furious. He vowed to make Sorelli suffer."

"Does Sorelli know about this?"

She shook her head. "I guess he assumed Cubby would accept losing the job. But he *hasn't* accepted it, Zack. That's what's so disturbing."

"And now for our first act, Zachary 'Zen' Freedman!" announced Sorelli.

Even with my cue, I didn't like to leave Whitney. She was pale, and her dark eyes were round and frightened, like she'd said too much. I felt bad. She seemed to be taking the superstition seriously.

On an impulse I said, "Stick around for my act. I'll work up a new bit, just for you."

As I ran out into the ring, I wondered what this new part of the act would be. I'd come up with something. I had to cheer Whitney up.

I also wondered if she was scared by the idea of a curse, or if she was scared of Cubby.

I started with a simple juggling pattern, a *cascade*. I tossed three clubs. They are the same shape as bowling pins, but in juggling, the term is clubs. Go figure.

Whenever I had a club in each hand, the third club in the air above them was at its highest point. In that instant, the clubs formed the three points of a triangle. People think of juggled objects as moving in circles, but it's a triangle shape.

I was focused on precision. I was in my own space again, in the world, but somehow away from it. It was just me and the clubs, flowing on and on.

As ours was a youth circus, the ringmaster kept the acts fairly simple. There was no flame-throwing on the trapeze swings, no sword-swallowing on the high wire. The dangerous tricks were for adult performers in the professional circuses. Sorelli said our concern was getting things right, not getting fancy.

The problem was, I was bored with tossing only three clubs. I could handle more.

I wanted to show off. Whitney was watching in the shadows, and I'd promised her something extra.

I called, "Hey, star gymnast. Bring my bag. I need more than three clubs. This is kid stuff."

The audience laughed and applauded. This was totally unscripted. After the show, Sorelli would be on my case big-time. But I didn't care.

Whitney carried my gym bag into the spotlight. I asked her to take two clubs out and put them under my chin.

I kept tossing the first three clubs. I caught the next one coming down in my right hand, as usual. Then, after passing it into my left hand, I dropped the two new clubs from under my chin into my right hand. I did this in the nanosecond before catching the next of the original three clubs.

I introduced a fourth club into the throws. I waited till I worked the four clubs into a smooth flow. Then I introduced the fifth.

The audience roared. They stood up to clap. Another standing O!

I was thrilled, but I didn't let it distract me. I kept the five clubs going, catching with the right as they fell and transferring to the left.

I was interrupted by loud frantic barking.

Pooch ran into the ring.

The audience screamed with laughter. I let the clubs complete their arcs. One by one, they plunked into my right hand.

I glared at Pooch. He'd ruined my act.

The dog ran in a circle around me, barking. He was pleased with himself for tracking me down.

The rope I'd tied him up with was still attached to his collar. It trailed behind him as he ran.

He hadn't escaped by chewing through the rope, or wriggling out of it.

So, how had he gotten free?

I dropped the clubs into my gym bag. Then I hoisted Pooch under my arm, grabbed my gym bag and marched out of the ring.

In the wings, the next performers up laughed. "You got a partner for your act, Zack," someone said.

Whitney said, "Pooch is so cute!"

"He is so going to the pound," I muttered back.

The ringmaster stomped out of his office. His face was boiling red, the same color as his jacket. "Zachary!"

Chapter Five

Sorelli ordered me outside. There he let loose a volley of yells that could be heard clear across the city. "First you ramp up your juggling act without permission. Then you set that animal on a *rampage!*"

He made it sound like Pooch was a dangerous beast of prey. At any other moment, this would have been funny.

"I'm sorry, sir. I had him tied up."
I glanced at Pooch, who was sniffing the flaps of the mess tent.

I thought of Thelma, shepherding hens back into the coop or barking her lungs out when she scented a coyote. Unlike Pooch, Thelma had been useful.

I told Sorelli, "Sir, I never even *wanted* this dog."

Sorelli opened his mouth for a fresh blast. Or so I assumed. Instead, the ring-master let out a huge sigh. He glanced from Pooch to me. For a second, I thought—ninth wonder of the world— he might smile.

Sorelli said gruffly, "Well, you may not like him, but he likes *you*. Get rid of him, Zachary. The dog goes, or you go."

He raised his voice to its regular multi-decibel pitch. "And no more funny stuff in the ring. I don't like funny."

He stomped back into the tent.

"You're hungry," I told Pooch shortly. "C'mon, we'll get you some grub."

I led him out of the circus, planning to stroll up to Fourth Avenue to find a corner store.

"Hey, Zack."

Cubby walked up to me, his red, two-foot-long clown shoes flopping. "Man, it's brutal getting bawled out by Sorelli."

Under his painted-on smile, Cubby had a broad grin. He was enjoying himself.

Then it hit me.

"You untied Pooch," I said.

Cubby's grin widened. "He looked so unhappy. I couldn't resist."

Couldn't resist sabotaging my act, he meant. I was cold with rage. I felt like grabbing him by the collar and hoisting him again. Only this time, I'd break his neck.

I squelched the impulse. Just. I said, "I'm taking Pooch to the pound tomorrow."

Cubby leaned his white-painted face with the huge, red-painted mouth close to Pooch. "So you're gonna be driving someone else crazy, huh?" He reached out a hand to pet him.

Pooch growled. He hadn't lost his dislike for Cubby.

Cubby drew back. Then he smirked at me. "Sorelli yelled at you, but he didn't kick you out. You're the teacher's pet. Everyone can tell."

I didn't think this was worth replying to, so I started to move away.

"Wait. I got something for you." Cubby fished in one of the deep pockets of his clown suit. He pulled out a pink leather leash with a matching collar. A large round metal medallion hung from the collar. One side of the medallion was speckled with tiny round holes.

He said, "I found this in the storage trailer. Circus Sorelli used to have a poodle act. I thought you could use it for Pooch."

He threw the leash to me. No, *at* me. I barely grabbed the collar before the medallion clipped me in the eye.

Cubby stalked toward the trailers, his big shoes flip-flopping.

Pooch and I stared after him. What a weird guy. Giving me the leash and collar should have been a friendly gesture.

But it hadn't come off that way.

Being a Vancouver girl, Whitney knew where the SPCA was. She, Pooch and I took the bus the next morning.

Pooch stuck his head out the window, a big, panting smile on his ugly face. I was sure he thought we were heading to a park for a nice walk.

We'd got permission from Sorelli to miss the 9:00 AM postmortem. That was where he played the DVD of the previous night's show and yelled at everyone.

I was still smarting from the reaming-out I'd received the night before. And this morning he'd topped it off with, "If I see that dog again, I will serve him up with mustard and relish."

I kept hold of Pooch, who was straining to jut his head farther out the window. Dumb dog. Any farther, and he'd fall out.

I remarked to Whitney, "Sorelli rarely finds fault with you, I've noticed. That's *something* to be said for the guy."

"Yeah, I guess." She pulled Pooch's ears back and wagged his head for him. He panted louder and smiled wider.

Whitney shrugged. "I come from a circus family. It's in my blood. I'm used to the beam, to practicing nonstop, that's all. I've been at it for years."

The bus ground to a stop at the crest of a big hill. The SPCA, a one-story building decorated with a mural of animals, was down the slope.

We got off, and Pooch trotted along happily. He wouldn't be so happy soon.

I didn't want to think about that, so I asked Whitney about her family.

She replied, "The circus goes way back with us. In the 1930s, my great-granddad was a farmer in Saskatchewan. The Depression wiped him out. So he joined a traveling circus. He did odd jobs: cleaning stables, taking tickets, whatever needed doing. Circuses were thriving then. No matter how bad the economy, people always grubbed pennies together to see the big show. After all, everybody loves a circus."

There was something in her tone, a flatness that puzzled me. "And how about you?" I asked.

Whitney hesitated. "Don't get me wrong. I like the circus. But what I'd really like is to try out for the Olympic gymnasts' team."

For a moment her face was hopeful. "I couldn't work for Sorelli anymore though. I'd have to concentrate on training."

I thought of Sorelli, expecting his performers to practice and work out seven hours a day. That was not only during circus season, but in the months leading up to it as well.

That didn't leave room for Olympic training. It didn't leave room for anything.

Halfway down the hill, Pooch stopped and sat down. Maybe all the cars rushing by were scaring him. I carried him the rest of the way.

I said to Whitney, "Why don't you quit then?"

Whitney grimaced. "Mom doesn't want me to. She's really into her society stuff: clubs, lunches, charity benefits, parties. If I were in Olympic training, she'd have to give a lot of that up. She'd have to travel around the country with me to meets and competitions.

"Dad says if I went for the Olympic team, he'd split the travel with Mom. But…" Whitney shrugged. "Mom shuts him down. She's the boss."

Pooch was whimpering. Now I got it. He recognized the SPCA building. It was the place Aunt Ellie had got him, the place he'd been kept in a cage.

Whitney scratched Pooch behind the ears. "What about you, Zack? You interested in a circus career?"

The image of Philippe Petit flashed into my mind. Petit wasn't much for circus performing. He liked to do things his own way.

"The circus is okay for now," I said lightly. "It beats my other option for a summer job—standing in front of my aunt's grocery store with a Buy Fresh Oranges sign."

Whitney laughed. She was pretty when she laughed. "You're a natural on the wire, Zack. And Sorelli likes you. That says a lot."

She was the second person to remark that the ringmaster liked me. Cubby had said it too.

But I knew Sorelli wasn't kidding about Pooch. *The dog goes, or you go.*

I thought of my chewed slippers and my ruined juggling act.

We walked inside the SPCA. At the sight of Pooch, a little girl jumped up and down like an out-of-control jack-in-the-box. "Wheee! Can I have that dog, Mommy? Can I?"

Her mom turned and smiled. It was a nice smile.

"You see, fella?" I murmured in Pooch's ear. "Everything's going to work out just fine."

Chapter Six

"I thought you were getting rid of that dog!"

The ringmaster loomed over me. Behind him, on the other side of the big top, was the massive cartoon of him on a billboard. The effect was scary. Kind of 3-D plus.

"Uhhh." I cleared my throat. I glanced down at Pooch. Unbothered by Sorelli, he was chewing the pink leash Cubby had given us.

"Well? Speak up, Zachary. What are you waiting for? Your old-age pension?"

"Uhhh. I tried to get rid of him, sir. Honest."

I couldn't explain what had happened, because I didn't really understand it myself. Maybe it was the jumpy kid. She made me nervous, and she might have made Pooch nervous.

Maybe I couldn't dump Pooch off the way orphaned kids got dumped off on relatives.

Sorelli narrowed his eyes. "You *tried* to? When I give an order, you don't *try*, Zachary. You *do*."

"Yes, sir."

"You think Philippe Petit thought about dogs when he walked the wire between the Twin Towers?"

How did Sorelli know I idolized Petit? I had never told him. The guy was uncanny.

I gulped. "No, sir. I'm sure dogs were not on Philippe Petit's mind."

"Exactly! And that's how it has to be in the circus. Your performance is everything. *You can have nothing else on your mind.*"

By now the whole of the Circus Sorelli company was gathered around, watching in wide-eyed terror. The ringmaster had a track record of reducing people to tears.

"Do you understand, Zachary?"

There was a silence. I could hear the Circus Sorelli flag flapping. Everyone held their breath the way the audience did when I was on the wire. In a way, I was on a high wire right now. If I made one wrong move, I'd be out of the circus.

I looked Sorelli in the eye. I said calmly, politely, "No, sir, I don't."

Sorelli's eyes bulged out of their sockets. He grabbed me by the elbow and marched me to his trailer.

Pooch trotted after us, still holding the pink leash in his mouth. The collar dragged behind him, bumping on the ground.

Sorelli's slam of the trailer door behind us echoed around the circus grounds.

"According to our permit, no animals."

"But doesn't that mean *performing* animals, sir? Pooch isn't a performer. He's a pet."

I noticed that Pooch had dropped the pink leash and collar. Now, in a corner of the trailer, he was fastening his jaw around one of Sorelli's shiny black boots. I picked him up.

"I've texted my aunt about Pooch. She'll take him when she gets back. It's just a few days, sir."

Sorelli plunged his big hairy hand into a box of tissues. Wrenching out half of them, he wiped the sweat off his face. "Last night Pooch wriggled out of his collar and ran to you, right in the middle of your juggling act. The city inspectors hear about that, they figure he's a performer. They revoke our permit and shut us down."

My shoulders sagged. I thought, *Sorry, Pooch. I tried.*

Sorelli pulled the remaining tissues out of the box. He mopped at a fresh outbreak of sweat on his forehead. "Besides, if I let you have a dog, every other performer and crew member will want a pet. Soon we'll be overrun with dogs, cats, lizards, birds, fish—"

"Okay, Mr. Sorelli," I interrupted, before he could go through the entire animal kingdom. "I'll find a home for Pooch."

"You have twenty-four hours. If the mongrel is still around, I replace you. Savvy? There's somebody else who's dying for the high-wire job."

Cubby, I thought. "Yes, sir."

The ringmaster gave me a phony smile that was scarier than any of his scowls. "Do you know why I'm giving you one more chance?"

"No, sir."

"Because I happen to like you. And Zachary?"

"Yes, sir?"

He glared at Pooch. "Get that mongrel out of my trailer!"

Whitney was waiting for Pooch and me outside. She lifted Pooch up and kissed his flabby face.

For such an ugly guy, he had all the luck.

We walked to the mess tent. We got a couple of Cokes for ourselves and filled a plastic cup with water for Pooch. Over his loud gulping, I related my conversation with Sorelli.

Whitney said, "Don't worry, Zack. If nothing else works out, he can stay with my parents till your aunt gets back."

I wondered how keen Whitney's mom would be to have a pup dumped on her. The Boothroyds sounded well off. They probably had a pretty nice place. Pooch might chew on their Ming vases or something.

"That'd be great," I said, not too hopefully.

"Mom will be at the show tonight. I got her a seat front row center." Whitney laughed. "You'll probably notice her. You can't miss Mom. No matter where she goes, she's always draped in bling! She says, what's the point in owning diamonds if you don't enjoy them?"

Whitney's gaze dropped to the pink leash and collar that I'd put on the table. She turned the collar over in her hands, studying the medallion.

I glanced around. Cubby was sitting with the other clowns, two tables away. They were wolfing down burgers.

He had his back to us, but I played it safe. I lowered my voice. "Clunky collar, huh? It's a gift from Cubby. He said it was once used in a poodle act."

Whitney cracked open the medallion to show me a couple of springs inside. "I've seen those poodle acts. You put a battery in here. Lights flash out the holes while the poodles parade around."

"Sounds hokey to me," I said.

"Welcome to the circus. Nothing is too hokey." She lowered her voice too. "Strange gift though."

"Strange guy."

Outside the mess tent, I picked up a stick. I started throwing it for Pooch to fetch. He brought it back every time. He was worry-free. That made one of us.

That evening, I left Pooch in the trailer during the show. Sorelli would have nothing to complain about. Both my wire and juggling acts would be seamless.

I climbed the ladder. On the ledge, I flexed my arms. I inhaled deeply and exhaled deeply.

I shifted my weight to my sides. I let go of all thoughts. My mind was clear as an Alberta summer sky.

I stepped on the thin black line. I started across, and soon I was one with the air.

There was the usual silence as people watched in awe. Then the silence was interrupted.

With a piercing scream.

What the—?

My skin tingled, a signal from my brain telling me it was curious. It wanted me to look down.

There was another scream.

The thought hammered at me: I had to see what was going on.

Distracted, I wavered.

The audience gasped. I was losing my balance. I was going to fall.

Chapter Seven

Distractions were no good. They pulled you down—on the wire and in life.

I clenched my arms, straining to keep my weight at my sides. I threw all thoughts overboard. I wouldn't look down. Nothing, nobody would get to me. I lifted my gaze so that the only thing I saw was the dark dome of the big top.

I was steady again. I kept going. My mind was blanker than it had ever been. I was lighter than I had ever been. I weighed nothing.

People were shouting at the screamer to be quiet. The audience was worried about me. They were indignant on my behalf. But I wasn't just seventy-five feet above them. I was an infinity away.

I reached the opposite ledge. The audience broke into wild applause.

Sorelli was climbing the ladder to greet me—a first.

Beaming, he hugged me. Over the applause, he shouted in my ear. "I've never seen anything like it. You kept your cool, even when that dame started screaming. You're a natural, Zen Freedman. You have a big future in the circus. Ringling, Cirque du Soleil… You'll be able to write your own ticket."

The audience, now standing, kept clapping, whistling and cheering.

"What was the screaming about?" I asked as I walked out of the ring with Sorelli. The strobe light stayed fastened on us.

"Wave!" Sorelli ordered me. He was grinning and bowing as we exited.

Through his grin, the ringmaster replied to my question. "Some dame got scared. It happens. The circus is intense for some people."

But when we pushed through the black curtain, we found a Circus Sorelli security guard trying to comfort a pale, shaking, middle-aged woman. "I came to the circus to enjoy myself—not be robbed!"

Beside the woman stood Whitney. Her dark eyes were wide and frightened.

Sorelli gaped from the woman to the security guard. "What's going on?" he bellowed.

The woman pulled aside the collar of her silk blouse to reveal a gash on her throat. "While I was watching this young man's act, someone behind tore my diamond necklace off my neck. When I turned, I saw a shadowy figure running up the aisle to the tent's entrance. The figure had a shawl over its head and shoulders—obviously as a disguise."

Sorelli's normally apple-cheeked face went gray. "A robbery at *my* circus? Madame, I'm—I'm—"

The woman snapped, "That necklace was an heirloom, Mr. Sorelli. Priceless. Irreplaceable! Yet when I tried to call for help, people yelled at me to be quiet. Hmph! So much for helping a citizen in distress."

"Erm, Madame…" The ringmaster loosened his shirt collar. He seemed to be having trouble breathing. "You didn't *say* anything. You just screamed. We didn't know that you'd been—"

Another type of scream, this one from a siren close by, interrupted him.

The woman gave a thin, bitter smile. "We'll see what the police have to say about this, Mr. Sorelli. And the mayor, for that matter. I have influence in this city. Circus Sorelli isn't safe. I'm going to see that it's shut down."

Everyone gasped. Whitney burst into tears. Sorelli went even grayer. I hoped he wasn't going to have a heart attack.

The wailing siren prompted another sound: loud barking from my trailer.

Sorelli whipped around to glare at me. His fury at Pooch restored some of the color to his cheeks. "That dog goes on the barbecue. Now."

Whitney placed a hand on the woman's silk-sleeved arm. "Please don't shut Circus Sorelli down. *Please*, Mom."

The next morning, before the post-mortem, everyone huddled around copies of the *Vancouver Sun*. The air in the big top grew heavier as we read.

Circus Becomes a Zoo
Anger and fear as necklace theft disrupts performance

A well-known socialite is vowing to shut Circus Sorelli down after a diamond necklace was torn off her neck.

"It's an outrage," Betty Boothroyd fumed of the theft, which occurred during last night's show. "Citizens should be able to go out without being terrorized. I'm contacting the mayor. I want Circus Sorelli's license revoked."

The Circus's second act was interrupted as police swarmed through the grounds and big top, seeking witnesses to the theft. Several people reported seeing a shawled figure flee from the tent.

After last evening's events, some circus-goers said they'd be too afraid to return. Boothroyd has gone a step further. She's withdrawing her daughter Whitney, a gymnast, from the show.

"If audience members aren't safe, performers aren't either," Boothroyd snapped.

But some Vancouverites may be too curious to stay away. In perhaps the most surprising development, high-wire walker Zack Freedman managed to keep his balance and finish his act despite the uproar below.

"Way to go, Zack," a few kids murmured. Others nodded.

We were all too shocked to say much. Would Whitney's mom really be able to shut us down?

I found Whitney. She was even more miserable, if that was possible, than the rest of us.

"I wanted to get away from the circus, Zack. But not like this," she said.

"Not in the middle of the season—if we even *have* the rest of the season."

Her eyes were full of tears. "I can't believe Mother would go this far. It's so unfair to everyone here."

Sorelli walked into the big top. He didn't have his usual brisk, impatient step. He looked defeated.

He inserted the DVD of last night's show into the player. He said nothing as the acts rolled on, even when Whitney flubbed her landing, or one of the clowns knocked over the can of yellow paint instead of plunging into it headfirst. Or later, when one of the trapeze artists missed connecting with her partner on the opposite swing and fell into safety net. Sorelli understood everyone had been knocked off their stride.

Sorelli did manage a crooked smile when my high-wire act came on. "Zen Freedman strikes again," he said.

He paused. He spoke in a quiet, very un-Sorelli-like voice. "The police have asked me to tell everyone that they want to search the grounds—including our trailers.

"They think the robbery may have been an inside job."

Chapter Eight

During the day, performers took turns practicing in the ring, because it could only hold so many of us. When we weren't in the ring, we were expected to work out.

I decided to go for a jog. I'd take Pooch with me.

When I returned to the trailer to get Pooch, Cubby was in his bathrobe.

He'd finally showered off the remains of the clown goop. He was holding the pink leash and collar high, and Pooch was jumping at it. I guessed Pooch was so excited by the idea of a walk, he'd forgotten his dislike for Cubby.

"You missed the postmortem," I said to Cubby.

"I decided to miss Sorelli spouting off this once."

Cubby teasing Pooch bugged me. I grabbed the leash out of his hand. "Sorelli said the cops were going to search everyone's trailer for the stolen necklace. They think it was an inside job."

"An inside job," Cubby snickered. "Aren't you Mr. *CSI*."

He turned and riffled through his chest of drawers for some clothes. He obviously wasn't worried about a search.

I tossed the leash on my bunk. I went outside, Pooch following.

I was on the other side of the big top, heading to the gate, when it occurred to me that Cubby's reaction to news of the police search was odd.

Cubby not only wasn't worried about a search—he hadn't been surprised by it.

The rest of us were pretty cheesed about the cops going through our stuff. Maybe Cubby didn't care.

Or maybe…he'd *expected* a search.

I paused in the middle of the concession area. Not understanding the delay, Pooch ran around me, panting.

If Cubby had expected a search, that could mean he'd been involved in the necklace theft. He could have been the shadowy figure.

No, that was crazy. Cubby was sore about losing the wire act. He was resentful and hostile. That didn't make him a thief.

Still…

I started walking again, Pooch trotting happily beside me. I wasn't so happy.

I was remembering yesterday afternoon in the mess tent. Cubby had been in earshot when Whitney described her diamond-flashy mother and mentioned exactly where she'd be sitting.

Cubby wanted revenge on Sorelli. He wanted to humiliate the ringmaster as Sorelli had humiliated him. This would have been the perfect way.

My mind ticked on, working out the possibilities.

Before the clown act, Cubby would have had time—just—to zoom out of the performers' area and into the big top. Everyone's eyes were glued to me on the high wire. Cubby could have raced up behind the unsuspecting Betty Boothroyd, wrenched the necklace off and escaped.

At the gate, a security guard was talking to a police officer. After a few minutes, the officer closed his notebook and walked away.

I went over to the guard. He was a young guy, only a few years older than me.

"Hey, Joel. Anything new on the necklace robbery?"

Joel turned and spat into the bushes by the fence. "Nothing yet. But the way that cop was grilling me, you'd think I was a side of beef. I thought this would be nice summer gig. Fresh air, sunshine, smiling faces…" He glanced up at the Circus Sorelli billboard. "The *Be Happy* place. Right."

Pooch had wandered into the trailer the guards used as an office. He was sniffing at a knapsack. Joel's lunch, no doubt.

And now Pooch's teeth were closing in on one of the knapsack's straps.

"Get out of there!" I called, annoyed.

Joel laughed. "Aw, he's okay."

I glanced around. The cop was still in sight talking on his cell phone.

I asked Joel, "Why do the police think somebody at Circus Sorelli was involved?"

Pooch ran out to us. I picked him up to avoid any further property damage.

In a low voice, Joel explained, "The cops interviewed the guard who was on duty last night. When he heard the screams, he headed to the big top. He saw a shadowy figure sprint out of the big top, someone wrapped in a shawl.

"Whoever it was headed straight for the performers-and-crew-only area. They unlocked the gate and went in."

Joel finished uneasily, *"The thief is one of us, Zack."*

Chapter Nine

Pooch and I reached Kits Beach. I started jogging. The sand pulled at my feet, slowing me down. It was a good workout. It was what I needed, a break from my problems. And boy, did I have problems—enough to fill a three-ring circus.

Problem one was the idea that Cubby might be the necklace thief. I couldn't shake it.

Problem two was that I had to find a home for Pooch until Aunt Ellie could pick him up.

I glanced down at Pooch. He was running with his tongue hanging out. I hoped he wouldn't forget his tongue was outside his mouth and bite it.

"You can look as goofy as you want. I can't keep you," I informed him.

Problem three was that Whitney was going to be yanked out of the circus by her mom. I would miss Whitney. I liked her. A lot.

Joel was right. Some *Be Happy* summer this was turning out to be.

I ran faster, Pooch puffing behind me. My head started to clear. I realized that Sorelli was the hardest hit by the necklace scandal. He might lose his circus. For me, Circus Sorelli was a cool summer gig. For him, it was everything.

I remembered how Sorrelli had played the DVD of last night's performance and barely watched it. All those flubs, and he hadn't said a word.

Maybe he'd felt there was no point. Maybe he believed Betty Boothroyd would really shut us down.

I stopped. Something was knocking at the edges of my mind. Something bothered me, but I wasn't sure what.

Pooch stopped, too, and looked at me inquiringly. Then he ran into the water for a drink. The *salt* water. Dumb dog.

I whistled for him—*Hooo-eee!*

When he trotted back to me, I said, "You want to make yourself sick?"

I led Pooch away from the beach and into a park. I tried to figure out what was nagging at me.

I mentally rewound. I'd been thinking of the postmortem. Specifically—

The DVD.

Was it something I'd seen on the DVD? Something from last night's show?

The problem was that I hadn't paid much attention to the DVD. None of us had. We were all feeling too stressed.

I flashed back over what I could remember. The moment Betty Boothroyd screamed. All the performer flubs after that.

I paused my memory on Cubby. I recalled his garish leer, his ghostly painted skin.

I shut my eyes, replaying Cubby's part in the clown act.

His performance had been seamless.

Maybe that's what was bothering me. After the scream, everyone had botched their act.

Not Cubby.

Maybe Cubby was the show-must-go-on type who kept his cool. Maybe that's why his performance had been flub-free.

But the more I thought about it, the less I saw it that way.

Say Cubby had stolen Mrs. Boothroyd's necklace. He'd done what he set out to do. He had humiliated Sorelli. He'd got his payback.

He'd been too pleased with himself to make mistakes.

When I got back to the Circus Sorelli gate, Joel told me to hurry inside. The security guard looked scared. "You weren't supposed to leave the grounds," he said. "Nobody is, till the cops finish searching. If Sorelli finds out, it'll be my job."

"Sorry," I said. "I didn't think."

It was getting close to my practice time in the ring. I got my stuff together, left Pooch in the trailer and headed to the big top.

In a while, I'd walk the wire. For a warm-up, I clomped around on stilts. Using the stilts toughened my leg muscles at the same time as I worked on balance.

Whitney was practicing on the balance beam. I strode over. By pressing my heels down on the stilt footholds, I was able to stand without falling.

I watched Whitney chalk the soles of her feet and palms of her hands. The beam was leather-covered. In the old days, it would have been polished wood, which is much more slippery. The leather cover made it easier for gymnasts.

The beam was still a tough act though, not unlike the wire. The beam was four inches wide, not much more than the wire's half-inch width. As with the wire, you had to concentrate to stay on the beam. With every leap, turn and somersault, you had to end up straight.

Whitney leaped. She did the splits, in a perfect parallel to the beam. Landing neatly, she spun without missing a beat into three midair somersaults.

She was good. No wonder Sorelli rarely found fault with her in postmortems.

She straightened out of the somersaults, landing feet together on the mat. She raised her arms in a graceful arc so that her palms met over her head.

"Perfect," I said.

She gave a wan smile. "Hey, Zack. I'm getting one last practice in—for old time's sake, I guess. Mom's coming to get me this afternoon."

I couldn't help thinking it: *And all because of Cubby Donnell.*

I blurted, "What if the police caught the thief? Would she let you stay?"

"What?!" Whitney stared at me, then laughed. "The air up there is making you light-headed, Zack."

I dismounted from the stilts so I could speak in a low voice. "I think I know who did it. I'm going to share my suspicions with Sorelli."

Whitney's dark eyes searched my face. She still looked disbelieving. "Well…she *might* let me stay. Gosh, Zack, that would be amazing."

I propped the stilts at ringside. I started walking away.

She called, "Wait! I have good news about Pooch. Mom agreed to take him till your aunt comes home."

I waved to show I'd heard. I was in too much of a hurry to answer.

I had to get hold of that DVD and watch it to make sure I was right.

Chapter Ten

The ringmaster smiled down at Pooch. Not a warm smile, but a smile. "I understand this little guy has a home. Whitney told me. Come on in."

He held open his trailer door.

"Not a home. A place to stay for a few days," I corrected. The idea of Pooch—and his chewing habits—at Betty Boothroyd's house was already making me uneasy.

Sorelli sighed. "I'm sorry to lose Whitney. On the other hand, I know she wants to try out for the Olympics. Well, she's got her wish now!" He gave a bark of bitter laughter.

Thinking the ringmaster was playing, Pooch barked back.

Sorelli scowled at him. "Is that dog being funny?"

"No, sir," I said quickly. "Uh, I was wondering if I could borrow—"

But Sorelli was busy pointing to the sparkly red uniforms hanging in his closet. "The kid wants the Olympics? She can have them! My life is that ringmaster's uniform. I got seven of 'em, one for each day of the week. Know why?"

"Er, no, sir."

"Because during every show, I sweat that uniform right through. When I take one of those babies off, it's dripping, Zachary. Dripping!"

"Sir, I—"

Sorelli was shaking his fist and yelling now. "I put my all into every show. I love the circus."

He let out a long breath and sank into a chair. He went on, "Every ringmaster is a showman through and through. We have to be larger and louder than anyone else. It's a tradition that goes back to George Claude Lockhart in Blackpool, England. It was the First World War, and people weren't going to the circus. Lockhart realized that, to attract people, you had to *dis*tract 'em. Make 'em forget reality. Give 'em sparkle, magic."

I knew Sorelli was thinking about how his own circus was threatened. Letting him talk might make him feel better. I listened.

Sorelli said, "It's a circus legend that old George Lockhart watches over us. Like a friendly ghost, he lingers among the shadows in his red duck-tail jacket..."

Just then, in the closet, Sorelli's red jackets started rustling.

Sorelli blanched, but I had a pretty good idea who our ghost was.

I walked over to the closet and pulled Pooch out by the scruff of his neck.

His teeth were clamped deeply into one of the ringmaster's shiny black patent-leather shoes. I gently pried it loose. "Sorry, sir."

Sorelli frowned at me. "What was it you wanted to borrow, Zachary? Money?"

"No, sir. I was wondering if I could have a look at last night's DVD."

"What? Ah." He smiled knowingly. "You want to admire yourself."

"That's not exactly it, sir…"

The ringmaster fished the DVD out of a bookcase. "I understand performers. You're all the same," he said. "Massive egos."

I let it go and headed back to my trailer.

When I got there, Cubby was opening the trailer door. He was going out. Good. I preferred not having him around while I watched the DVD.

As I walked up the trailer steps, I knew I was scowling, but I didn't change my expression. I couldn't be bothered.

Cubby swung the door so wide, it hit me.

I grabbed him by the wrist. "I know what you are, *Jacob*. A thief. You stole Mrs. Boothroyd's necklace. You just had to mess things up for Sorelli—for everyone."

Cubby pulled away from me. He looked surprised, but he quickly covered it with a smirk. "Can't prove it though, can you?"

He sauntered off.

Cracking open a Coke can, I slumped down on my bunk and slid the DVD into my laptop.

When the knock at the door came, it startled me.

"Hey, Zack."

Whitney shaded her eyes and peered through the screen. "I thought maybe I should take Pooch to my trailer. Mom will be here soon."

Pooch was up on his hind legs, front paws flat against the door. He liked Whitney. As opposed to Cubby, whom he couldn't stand.

As judges of character, Pooch and I were pretty much on par.

I stared stupidly at Whitney. My mind was still on the DVD. I'd watched Cubby perform his clown act after Betty Boothroyd's scream. I'd been right. He hadn't missed a beat—not like other performers. They'd had flub after flub.

I thought of my run-in with Cubby earlier. It bothered me. I shouldn't have lost it like that. I shouldn't have let Cubby get to me, no matter what.

I shut the laptop. "Sorry—you were talking about Pooch. Yeah, of course. I'll get his stuff together for you."

Still, I didn't move. I'd been waiting to be free of Pooch. But now that the moment was here, I felt almost…lonely.

That was dumb, I reminded myself. Pooch couldn't stay here.

Besides, I didn't need anyone. I was Zack Freedman. I could get by on my own.

Whitney stepped inside and began fussing over Pooch. She scratched his ears and head and cooed at him. The little guy lapped it up.

She'd be good to him, I knew that. Then, in a few days, Aunt Ellie would find another home for Pooch.

I fished my Circus Sorelli bag out of a drawer. Every performer and crew member got one. They were cloth bags decorated with—you guessed it— Sorelli's beaming face.

I put the dog-food tins inside. I added a nylon rope that Pooch liked to chew on.

I didn't look at him. Handing the bag to Whitney, I explained, "I give him half a tin in the morning, half in the evening. He finished off a tin this morning."

Whitney took the bag. She looked at me doubtfully. She could see I didn't feel good about this.

What I didn't feel good about was the DVD. I wanted to talk to her about what I'd seen on it. But I knew I should go to Sorelli first.

So all I said was, "Please thank your mom for taking Pooch."

Pooch didn't want to go with Whitney. He hung back, head tipped to one side, watching me. In the end, I had to fasten the nylon rope around him so Whitney could lead him away.

I listened to Pooch's claws scrabble on the trailer steps. I watched him and

Whitney walk to her trailer. I had that lonely feeling again.

Then I had a different feeling, a sense that I'd forgotten something when I packed up the bag.

That couldn't be. All Pooch had were those dog-food tins I'd bought him.

Wait. That wasn't all Pooch had.

Draped over the end of my bunk was Cubby's gift to Pooch, the pink leash. And its matching collar with that clunky medallion.

There was no point in sending them with Whitney. They were useless to Pooch. What an idiot Cubby had been, thinking any owner would put that stuff on a dog.

Not that I was Pooch's owner, I corrected myself—

And then there were more knocks on the door, this time louder and heavier.

"Open up. This is the police."

Chapter Eleven

There were two police officers. One of them asked me to step outside and gave me a pat-down while the other stomped inside the trailer. I heard him going through Cubby's and my stuff. I heard lots of crashes.

"Uh—I left my laptop in there," I began uneasily.

The first officer ignored that. He asked me for my name and the name of the guy I roomed with.

It occurred to me that I hadn't seen Cubby for a while. He was conveniently missing this body search.

"I'm Zack Freedman. The other guy is Cubby Donnell."

The officer glanced at me. He'd noticed how my tone changed, grew hostile, when I said Cubby's name. I hadn't intended it.

"We've already seen Cubby," the officer said.

He took a list of performers and crew out of his pocket. He ticked my name off. I saw a checkmark beside Cubby's name too.

The other cop came out. They headed to the next trailer.

I went back inside. Bedsheets were bundled up and dumped on top of dressers. Clothes lay all over the floor.

Entwined in them were the pink leash and collar.

I started cleaning up my side of the trailer. Let Cubby clean up his own side.

Loud barking interrupted me.

Pooch was sounding the alarm. The cops must be going through Whitney's trailer.

I ran outside. Whitney was standing with her roommates.

She explained, "I'm not allowed to leave till they search my stuff."

I walked up the steps and peered in. Pooch was lying beside the Circus Sorelli cloth bag. One of the cops tried to reach for the bag to check inside. Pooch growled.

I whistled to Pooch. With a resentful glance at the cop, he trotted outside with me. The cop glanced into the bag, snorted and tossed it aside. One dog's treasure was another man's garbage.

Whitney told me, "You'll have to come visit Pooch."

Then she smiled, and I knew she meant *visit Pooch and me.*

Any other day, I would have felt like I could walk on air—without the help of a wire.

But this wasn't any day.

I recalled what I'd seen on the DVD. I needed to talk to Sorelli before it was too late.

I'd thought I wouldn't have to. I'd hoped the cops' search of our trailers would turn up the necklace—and reveal the thief's identity.

I looked around. Other performers and crew stood waiting for the police to finish their search. Everybody was sullen and silent. The whole procedure was pretty insulting.

So where was Cubby?

He couldn't have left the grounds. Joel would have stopped him. And even if he had snuck out, it would be like putting a large neon question mark over his head. Sorelli would find out he was missing. The cops would zero in on him.

I was sure Cubby didn't want that.

The two officers bounded out of Whitney's trailer. They pushed on to the next one.

I took Whitney's hand in mine. I couldn't think of any girl I'd ever liked more. All I wanted to do was stay beside her.

But I had a thief to catch.

"I have to go talk to Sorelli," I said.

I played the DVD for Sorelli. I showed him the part that bothered me— the puzzle piece that didn't fit.

"You crazy, Zachary? That proves nothing!"

Still, he grabbed a handful of tissues and mopped at his forehead. He kept staring at the laptop.

He let out a huge sigh. "Under the circumstances, the behavior is a *little* weird, I'll give you that. But we need more than that to bring charges. We need proof, Zachary!"

Outside, Pooch heard Sorelli yelling. He started to bark. I bit back a smile. Pooch assumed Sorelli wanted to play.

"That mongrel is *still* here?"

"Whitney's about to take him away," I assured Sorelli.

But not yet, I thought. *She can't leave yet. Not before I tell her that I—*

Care about her?

I wondered if I could get the words out. Me, a simple ranch kid from Alberta.

The cops were barging into another trailer. Meanwhile, Whitney emerged from hers with her suitcase and the cloth bag. Pooch trotted after her. I watched him through the window, sniffing at the bag.

Every once in a while, Pooch forgot his stomach and glanced around. I guessed he was wondering about me. He couldn't understand why I'd abruptly vanished from his life.

Whitney saw me in the window. She hesitated, unsure whether to wait. Then, with an apologetic shrug, she started walking to the big top. She'd arranged to meet her mom inside.

Just then, Cubby came out of the big top. He put his thumbs in his ears and waggled his fingers at Pooch.

Pooch just stared at him, astonished.

From here, I could read Cubby's lips. *Wait*, he told Whitney.

Cubby sprinted to our trailer. A moment later he ran out, brandishing the pink leash and collar. He dangled it above Pooch, just a little too high.

Pooch had been sniffing at the cloth bag again. Now he started jumping, trying to clamp his teeth around the collar.

Quite the sense of humor Cubby had.

But I wasn't so concerned with Cubby's personality at the moment. I was more interested in the collar that he was waving around.

Behind me, Sorelli slammed his palm down on his desk. "You're not listening to me, Zachary. Maybe your ears need de-waxing? I'm telling you that your theory isn't enough. We need proof."

"Yeah," I agreed absently.

As Cubby waved the collar above Pooch, I watched how the sun caught on the big, round metal medallion.

The big, round, *hollow* metal medallion.

Chapter Twelve

Cubby could have stolen the necklace—and stashed it inside the medallion. The perfect hiding place.

When the cops searched our trailer, they wouldn't have paid attention to a dog's leash and collar.

That would explain why Cubby was so calm about the search. He was a hundred percent sure no one would crack open the medallion and check inside.

Images spooled through my mind. All of them starred Cubby, and none of them were pleasant.

Cubby resenting the ringmaster and vowing revenge. Cubby being hostile to me from day one.

Cubby shoving his clown face with its garish paint up close to Pooch. Scaring Pooch.

I smiled at that. Pooch had scared Cubby right back with his angry barking. Pooch sure didn't like Cubby.

At that thought, a light switch flicked on in my mind. I saw Cubby through Pooch's eyes, and I understood.

Outside, Whitney started walking toward the big top again. Pooch followed, still sniffing the cloth bag.

Cubby stuffed the leash and collar back into his sweatpants pocket.

He headed for the gate that led to the public area.

I had to act quickly. If I didn't, the thief would escape the circus grounds with the diamond necklace.

I charged out the door.

I ran toward Cubby. The other performers and crew members, standing around while the police did their searches, watched me in astonishment. Their heads swiveled as I ran, as if they were following a ball in a tennis game.

The cops, who were exiting another trailer, saw me too. Instantly they were suspicious. "Hold on there, sonny," one of them called.

I knocked against Cubby. He leaped back, rubbing his arm.

"Hey, what's the big idea?" he demanded.

I didn't reply. I kept going.

"*Whitney.*" I grabbed her by the elbow. I pulled her behind the big top, out of everyone's view. If I could just have a minute alone with her. A half-minute.

"What are you doing, Zack?"

She didn't get that I'd figured it out. She set her suitcase down and smiled at me. Her dark eyes were warm and trusting.

I urged, "You still have a chance. Go to Sorelli, now. Give him the necklace. We'll work something out with him. Somehow we'll manage it. No one will know."

Shocked, she hesitated. I saw the doubt in her face.

Then the warmth went out of her eyes. "I have no idea what you're talking about."

I heard footsteps pounding the grass behind us. The cops were almost here.

"Please, Whitney. *I know you stole your mom's necklace.* You said it yourself:

if there was no Circus Sorelli, your dad would find a way to get you to Olympic training."

Pooch was sitting, looking happily up at me. His tail wagged.

Whitney wrenched her arm free. "Don't be stupid. It's Cubby who has the grudge against Sorelli."

The two police officers bounded up behind us, followed by Sorelli. Performers and crew crowded up behind.

Talk about a circus.

"That doesn't prove I took my mom's necklace," Whitney insisted.

"Maybe not," I agreed. "But I have other proof."

Sorelli flapped his hands at the performers and crew. "Show's over, everyone. Get out or you're all fired."

They trickled away reluctantly.

The cops were scowling—at me, not Whitney. One of them warned,

"You're interfering with an investigation, young man."

I kept looking at Whitney. "The DVD of last night's performance," I said. "There was something about it that bothered me. At first I thought it was Cubby. Then I watched it again and realized it was you.

"You were clumsy on the beam. Perfect you. Something had to be making you nervous."

"Everyone was nervous," Whitney protested. "After my mom screamed, we were all off."

I nodded. "Sure we were—those of us who were on after your mom screamed. *But you came on before*."

The cops swung their gazes to Whitney.

I said, "You were jittery because you were about to steal the necklace. You weren't sure you'd get away with it. You had the thief's version of stage fright."

Whitney's grip tightened on the cloth bag. Pooch, who'd been sniffing at the bag some more, sat back and looked at her curiously.

"That still doesn't prove anything," she said and turned to the officers with a hard little smile. "Does it?"

Their expressions were unreadable. I guessed they were trained not to show reactions.

"You searched my trailer," Whitney reminded them. Her voice was gaining confidence now. "You found nothing. I can go."

She hoisted her suitcase.

The cops glanced at each other. They exchanged the faintest of shrugs.

They stood back, allowing Whitney to pass.

"Just a minute," I said.

Before she could stop me, I grabbed the cloth bag from her hand.

"While searching Whitney's trailer, you checked this out?" I asked the cops.

"Yeah," one shrugged. "Bunch of dog-food tins."

"Value-added dog-food tins," I said.

Chapter Thirteen

I turned the cloth bag upside down and dumped the tins on the ground.

Whitney's dark eyes were blazing. She was scared and angry.

"Four tins," I said. "That's what I gave you earlier today. Four *unopened* tins of dog food."

I bent down and picked up an opened tin with plastic wrap around the top.

Whitney dropped her suitcase and started to run. One of the cops side-stepped, blocking her. "Not so fast, miss," he said pleasantly. "Let's see what our junior detective has to show us."

I stuck my hand into the cold, wet goop of dog food in the opened tin. I drew it out again.

Even with globs of dog food covering it, the diamond necklace winked and glistened in the afternoon sun.

One of the cops finally reacted. His jaw dropped. "Well, I'll be durned. This young fella really is a junior detective."

"Not me." With my other hand I pointed to Pooch. "He was the one who gave Whitney's hiding place away. He kept sniffing at the bag. It was a tip-off to me that not all the cans were sealed."

"Right up to the end, I thought Cubby was the thief," I told Sorelli. "I was so *sure*.

He was bitter over losing the wire job. He was hostile to me. Then there was that stupid pink collar with the hollow medallion—the perfect hiding place…"

The ringmaster and I were sitting in his office. The police were questioning Whitney at the station. Nobody thought Mrs. Boothroyd would press charges, so Whitney probably wouldn't have to face a judge.

On the other hand, we had all got a taste of Betty Boothroyd's explosive temper when the necklace was stolen. Whitney would have to face that, which was maybe a worse punishment for her.

I sighed. "I didn't like Cubby. I couldn't accept that Cubby might have been trying to *help* Pooch. But, in his goofy way, he liked my dog. Even if, most of the time, Pooch didn't like him."

Sorelli nodded. "Cubby told me he'd borrowed the leash and collar from the storage trailer. Once he saw you weren't interested, he was going to return it. That's why he was carrying it around."

The ringmaster arched a thick black eyebrow at me. "Erm, Zachary...did I hear you say, *my* dog?"

I glanced at Pooch, who was asleep on the floor beside my chair. I shook my head. "Slip of the tongue, sir. I've had a text message from Aunt Ellie. She has a friend who wants a dog. Pooch would be the perfect companion for her. So"—I shrugged—"it's all taken care of."

"That's great, Zachary. Because you've got big things ahead of you. Like I always say, the circus has to be everything."

Then he scowled. The guy's moods were like a mixed sky: part sun, part storm clouds. "No more of this detecting stuff. No more crushes on girls—yes, I noticed you had a thing for Whitney. And no more pet dogs."

Wearily, I explained for the millionth time that Pooch hadn't been my idea.

Sorelli held up a hand. Mood change again—now he was beaming.

"Gonna be a big night tonight, Zachary. The capture of the thief has been all over the news. We've been rushed off our feet with calls for tickets. We're already setting up the cattle guard."

Cattle guard meant temporary low seats set up in front of the regular seats to accommodate an overflow audience. "That's great," I said.

"And, I got word that a talent scout from Ringling will be here. He's heard about you."

"That's great," I said again.

Sorelli looked at me. "You gonna be okay tonight? I know you took this Whitney thing pretty hard."

I thought of Whitney's so-dark eyes looking up at me. Trusting and warm, then cold and blank. I had no chance to tell her that I still cared, no matter what.

Yeah, I'd taken it hard.

But what else could I have done? If I hadn't revealed what I'd figured out, Whitney would have got away with the theft. Worse, suspicion might have fallen on Cubby.

I slumped back in my chair. No wonder I liked the wire so much. Up there, you escaped these kinds of complications.

"If only life were as simple as the thin black line," I muttered.

"What's that?" Sorelli leaned forward. "Speak up, son! You gonna be able to walk the line tonight?"

I looked at him in surprise. "Yeah, I can walk it, sir."

He sat back, satisfied. "That's my boy. That's my Zen Freedman talking."

I was on next. I waited by the black curtain. When the unicyclists finished, I'd go into the ring.

Cubby stood behind me, waiting with the other two clowns. He whispered, "So now you're a thief catcher as well as a wire star."

The guy was *still* needling me. I whipped around.

But, in the midst of his painted-on face, his eyes were friendly. He asked, almost shyly, "How's Whitney?"

I relaxed. "I dunno. I've tried calling, but she doesn't want to speak to me. Surprise, surprise."

Cubby nodded. "Sorry, Zack. I know you liked her."

From the other side of the black curtain, the packed audience burst into applause. It was just about my cue.

There was something I wanted to tell Cubby first. "Hey, Cub. Earlier today I was thinking about how Pooch sees you."

He looked down at his oversized clown shoes. "Not very favorably. Guess he just doesn't like me."

"No. Listen. Pooch doesn't like you when you're wearing that clown guck. But when you're cleaned up, he plays with you. He jumps for that pink collar."

The unicyclists pushed through the curtain. I needed to go on.

But Cubby was watching me, his eyes half dubious, half hopeful. "I don't get it."

"I finally figured it out," I told him. "Pooch has *coulrophobia*. Fear of clowns. People get it. Why shouldn't dogs?"

Chapter Fourteen

The cheering started when I climbed the ladder. I heard my name called over and over. That *Sun* story was building a rep for me.

I grinned. I basked in it. I got why people sweated out the hours of practice, the close quarters and having no life of their own. There was nothing like audience adoration.

I stood on the ledge. I took deep breaths.

I thought of Philippe Petit and his walk between the Twin Towers. The Towers weren't there anymore, but Petit's walk lived on in documentaries, books and paintings.

The police had warned Petit that the wire walk would be illegal. That didn't stop him. In fact, when he saw the police waiting for him at the other side, he jumped and danced on the wire to taunt them.

The guy was a rebel. He wrote a book about himself called *The Square Peg*. In other words, someone who doesn't fit in. Who does the unexpected.

Maybe that was what I most admired about Petit.

The audience was quieting down. They were waiting for me.

Somewhere down there was a talent scout. I wanted to show off to him, to cross that thin black line like I was one with the air.

I also wanted to please Sorelli. He'd been good to me. He believed in me.

I thought what a dream job this was. The alternative was standing outside Aunt Ellie's organic-foods store with a placard.

Pooch was back in the trailer. Tomorrow Aunt Ellie's friend would pick him up. I imagined this friend collecting Pooch, walking him out of my life. My exciting life, with big things ahead of me, like Sorelli said.

I stepped on the wire. My weight was at my sides. I was in control. I was Zen.

The audience was silent, holding its breath. They knew the safety net was below, but they were still scared for me. They'd relax only when I was almost to the other side.

I moved forward, my steps light, my footholds secure.

Again the image of Pooch flashed into my mind. Happy, trusting Pooch, trotting alongside me. I realized it: I'd kind of gotten used to the little mutt.

Kind of? Who was I kidding? I didn't want Aunt Ellie's friend to take Pooch away from me. Pooch was my dog.

But I couldn't keep him—as long as I stayed at Circus Sorelli.

Pooch, or the circus.

All at once the choice was as clear in my mind as a blue Alberta sky. I made my decision.

I moved forward. I missed my step. To the audience's gasps and shrieks, I fell down, down, into the safety net.

Two weeks later...

I stood outside Aunt Ellie's shop. I didn't wear a placard advertising fresh oranges. Instead, I juggled them.

Pooch ran around me, barking. He kept hoping one of the oranges would fall, so he could catch it. I never dropped one, but he never gave up. Dumb dog.

People stopped to watch us. It was kind of a double act.

It was about time for my break. I stopped juggling and grinned down at Pooch. "Okay, sport. Now we'll go to the park, and you can pretend you're scaring the ducks."

Down the sidewalk, a car door slammed.

"Zachary!"

Sorelli was stomping toward me. Instead of his red jacket and jodhpurs, he wore jeans and a T-shirt. But he was still larger than life. Heads turned as he passed.

"Hi, sir," I said uncertainly.

When I quit Circus Sorelli, I'd apologized to him for falling. For refusing to go back up on the wire.

He had yelled so long and so loudly, I hadn't been sure he'd heard.

I wondered if he was going to start yelling again now.

He didn't. He sank down onto the curb. I sat with him.

"You did it on purpose," the ringmaster accused. He glared at Pooch. "You fell so you could keep a *dog*."

I knew anything I said would just annoy him. So I started juggling the oranges again.

Sorelli fumed, using colorful language, for a while longer. Then he grew hot and wiped his face with the hem of his T-shirt.

"Here, sir." I handed him one of the oranges. "Have this. It'll cool you off."

Melanie Jackson is the author of numerous mysteries for youth, including *The Big Dip* and *Fast Slide* in the Orca Currents series, as well as the popular Dinah Galloway Mystery series. Melanie lives in Vancouver, British Columbia.

Titles in the Series

orca currents